W9-BZA-437

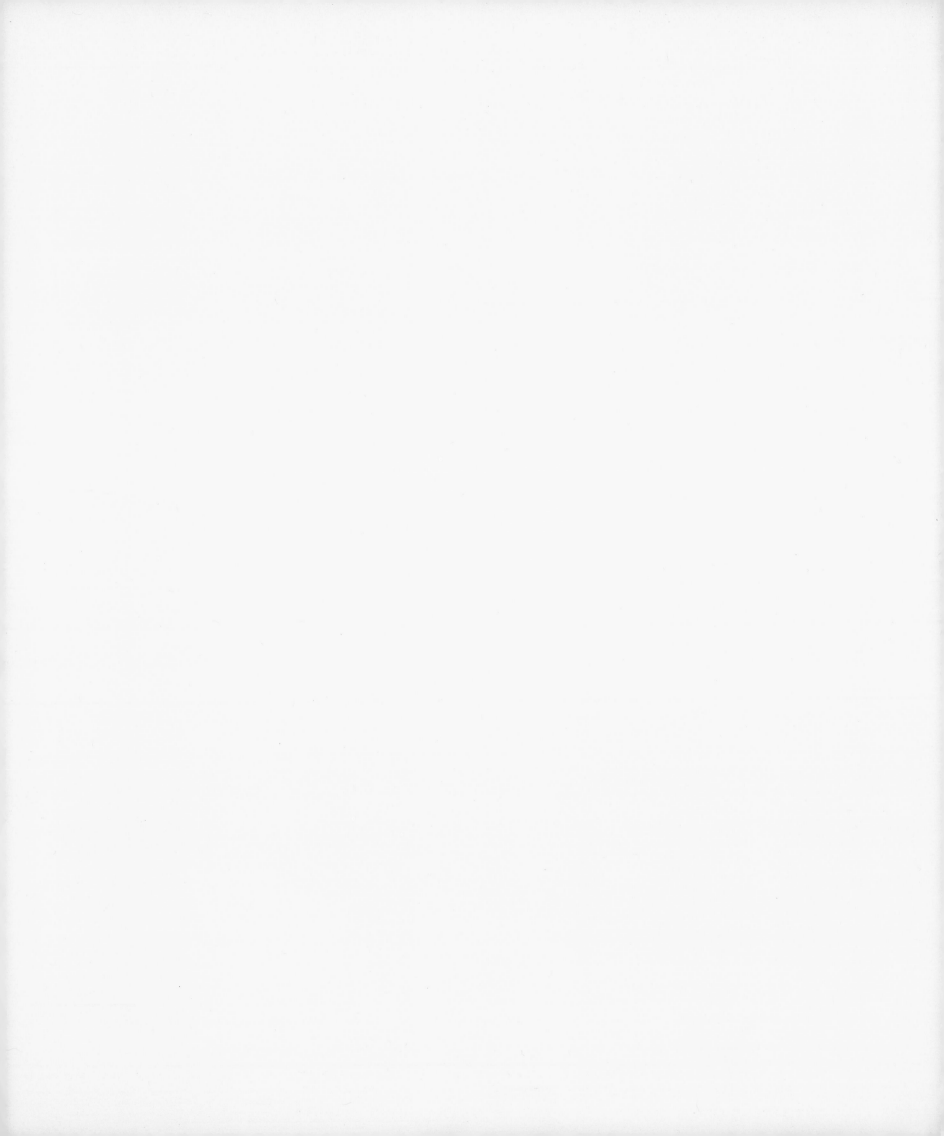

A Cowboy Christmas

THE MIRACLE AT LONE PINE RIDGE

BY **Audrey Wood**

PAINTINGS BY **Robert Florczak**

Simon & Schuster Books for Young Readers

NEW YORK LONDON TORONTO SYDNEY SINGAPORE

SIMON & SCHUSTER BOOKS FOR YOUNG READERS

An imprint of Simon & Schuster Children's Publishing Division

1230 Avenue of the Americas, New York, New York 10020

Text copyright © 2001 by Audrey Wood

Illustrations copyright © 2001 by Robert Florczak

All rights reserved, including the right of reproduction in whole or in part in any form.

SIMON & SCHUSTER BOOKS FOR YOUNG READERS is a trademark of Simon & Schuster.

2 4 6 8 10 9 7 5 3 1

Library of Congress Cataloging-in-Publication Data

Wood, Audrey.

A cowboy Christmas / by Audrey Wood ;

illustrated by Robert Florczak.—1st ed.

p. cm.

Summary: When Cully the cowboy, a friend and a father figure to Evan,

fails to show up at the ranch on an icy Christmas Eve,

Evan goes out into the night to find and rescue him.

ISBN 0-689-82190-5 (hc)

[1. Cowboys—Fiction. 2. Ranch life—Fiction. 3. Christmas—Fiction]

I. Florczak, Robert, ill. II. Title.

PZ7.W846Co 2000

[E]—dc21

98-36195

For Hank Bidgood
—A. W.

For Don Rohren, a cowboy at heart
—R. F.

The cowboy had stayed out too long on the winter range, chasing strays for extra cash. For seven years he had dodged the misfortunes of the trail, but now his luck was running thin. He was tired to the bone and a deep cough had settled in his chest.

He should have spent the night in town when he'd stopped to buy the burnished silver bridle that hung on his saddle horn. Instead, he'd pressed on toward the ranch where the boy and the widow were waiting. He tried to stay alert, but his head nodded as he drifted in and out of a feverish sleep.

As a half-moon arose, the sky cleared and the night grew colder. For miles his horse had been finding her own way, heading south. At the crest of Lone Pine Ridge, she reared as the cowboy slipped from his saddle and fell to the icy ground.

It was Christmas Eve at the small ranch below the ridge. Evan pressed his face against a frost-covered window pane and peered into the night. The cowboy had always returned to the ranch long before the first snow fell.

"Ma," he said, "Cully's never been this late before. What if something happened?"

"Now don't you fret," Della said, putting a Christmas pie into the oven. "Worrying won't help anything."

The boy watched the prairie wind whip the branches of a young scrub pine. When his father died, Evan helped his mother plant the seedling near the window. "To remember," his ma said.

Evan remembered.

That first summer had been the hardest. Evan missed his dad every day. Ma needed his help from dawn till dusk—there was never time to play, or ride off on his horse to explore the land.

If it weren't for the cowboy, that winter would have been even worse. Cully and Evan's pa had been best friends. Before he passed on, Evan's pa had asked his friend for a promise. Would he help out at the ranch through the cold months?

In December, Cully came back to the small ranch below the ridge and kept his promise. He worked all winter and stayed in the bunkhouse, and he had returned every winter since.

One Christmas, Cully brought Evan a rope.

"When cowboys sleep out on the range," he explained, "they make a circle out of a horsehair rope and lay their blanket inside it. No snake will cross over a horsehair rope."

After that, Evan lassoed his bed every night so he could sleep like a cowboy.

The next year, when Evan told his ma he wanted to tame a wild horse, she said he wasn't ready. But Cully thought differently.

"The boy's going to be running your spread soon enough, ma'am. I think he can break that filly if he has a mind to do it."

Evan smiled when he recalled that day. The horse had thrown him four times. He was scraped and sore, but Cully wouldn't let him give up, not even when the horse bucked him over the corral fence. The cowboy laughed until tears streamed down his face.

"I didn't know anything without wings could fly that far!" he exclaimed.

In the long winter evenings Evan and Della sat by the hearth and listened to the cowboy's tales of his life on the trail.

"After a long, hot ride we finally camped at Red River. Cookie had our beans boiling in the pot, when an ornery steer got stuck in a mud hole. No one wanted to get him out, so they volunteered me for the job. I lassoed him and my horse gave him a good pull. Now you'd think that longhorn would have been grateful, but when I set him loose, he chased me around camp like I was a Spanish matador. He finally stopped when a pretty heifer called him over for a kiss."

"Maybe that bull was just trying to say thank you," Evan said. "If you had stayed put he might have kissed you instead!" And the cowboy laughed.

The boy came to know all of Cully's friends through the stories he told. He longed to meet each one, and he always asked about them.

"What about Lucky Lefty? Was he with you this season?"

"Yep," Cully said. "And he's luckier than ever. One stormy day we were pushing the herd over Barker's Pass. Lucky and I were riding together, and to while away the time, he was telling the story of Noah and his animal ark. He was just to the part about the forty days and forty nights when, out of nowhere, prairie lightning flashed down from a cloud and struck him right on his chest."

"Was he hurt bad?" Evan asked.

"It knocked him straight off the back of his horse, but he lived. He's got a long scar to show where the lightning hit him . . . on his left side of course."

"Maybe the Lord didn't like the way Lucky was telling the story," Della said with a smile.

"I'll warn him about that, ma'am," the cowboy said, smiling back.

Most of the year, Evan's ma wanted him to go to sleep early so he could work better the next day. But when Cully was there, she often went to bed first, leaving them to talk late. That's when the cowboy told his most exciting stories.

"What about bears? They bother you much?" Evan asked.

"Only once, up north. We'd just finished our supper when a giant grizzly ambled into camp. It had been raining, and everyone had their guns stowed with their rain gear. Cookie saw him coming and ran like a fox, and the rest of us took off, too. The grizzly set right to work tearing into our chuck wagon. I knew we'd lose all of our supplies if somebody didn't do something, so I jumped on my horse and Hames got his horse. Now it wasn't easy, but we captured that bear with nothing but our lariats."

"Was he mean? Weren't you afraid?" Evan asked.

"He put up a fierce fight," Cully said. "But sometimes you have to do what has to be done. As we dragged him away from camp, he chewed through my rope and snapped Hames's rope like a thread."

"Did he chase you?" Evan wanted to know.

"Nope," Cully answered. "He just tucked his stubby tail down, ran off like a cub, and never came back."

Evan returned from his thoughts. Outside, the barn door flew open, banging against the building. The horses were frightened. It was time to take care of things. Grabbing a lantern, he said, "I'm going out to fix that door, Ma."

"Don't be long," Della called. "I could use some help getting Christmas dinner ready."

As he started toward the barn, the wind abruptly stopped blowing, like a candle flame being snuffed out. The boy's ears rang in the silence. He looked across the snowy valley, desperately hoping to spot a rider coming toward the ranch in the moonlight.

Evan had grown to love the cowboy, and he felt in his heart that something was wrong.

Looking up at the Christmas sky, he saw one star shining brighter than the rest. He thought about the miracle in Bethlehem and the star that the wise men had followed to find the newborn baby. "With faith all things are possible," his ma always said.

Evan closed his eyes, and prayed: *Father in Heaven, since Pa died I haven't talked to you much, so I hope that you are listening now. Watch over my friend Cully. Don't let anything bad happen to him, and please, bring him back home to Ma and me. That's all I want for Christmas. Amen.*

He was turning toward the barn when he noticed a silvery light on Lone Pine Ridge. The light rose up and hovered in the air. The boy scarcely breathed as he watched the mysterious light flicker, then fade away. Evan shuddered as an old saying sprang into his mind: If a cowboy dies alone on the range his soul will shoot to heaven like a star.

Della wondered why it was taking Evan so long to fix the barn door. She lit another lantern, and found her son leading his horse out of the corral.

"Evan!" she called. "What are you doing?"

"I saw a strange light on the ridge, Ma," he called back. "I think . . . maybe it's Cully."

The wind picked up and began to blow again.

"Saddle up, son," his ma said. "I'm going with you."

As they ran their horses across the valley, snow clouds were moving in from the north, swallowing the stars and the moon.

Spurring his horse hard, the boy led the way, racing up to the crest of the ridge. It was black as midnight in the pines. Evan relit the lanterns they had brought and handed one to his ma.

"Let's split up," he suggested, "like Cully and I do when we're tracking strays."

Snow began to fall, and the wind took on a deeper chill as they slowly rode their horses, searching the ridge.

An hour passed. Evan's teeth were chattering, and his hands were numb through his gloves.

"Son!" his ma called. "There's no one up here but us. We've got to get back to the ranch!"

We can't give up, he thought. *That light was a sign. I know it!*

Evan heard something that sounded like the scrape of a hoof against a rock. He slid off his horse quietly. The boy moved between the trees, listening, then searching whenever he heard the sound.

At last he came to an old scrub pine at the edge of the ridge. There he found a riderless horse standing with its back to the wind.

"Ma!" he shouted. "Over here! It's Cully's horse!"

Raising his lantern high, he peered into the night and saw a dark shape on the frozen ground.

"Ma!" he shouted again. "Hurry!"

Della rode over and jumped down from her horse.

"Is he breathing, Ma?" Evan asked.

Taking Cully's icy hand, Della felt for a pulse. Then she tore open his coat and pressed her ear to his chest, listening for a heartbeat. A low rattling sound came from the cowboy's throat.

"Ma?" Evan said.

"He may not make it, son," she answered. "Let's get him home."

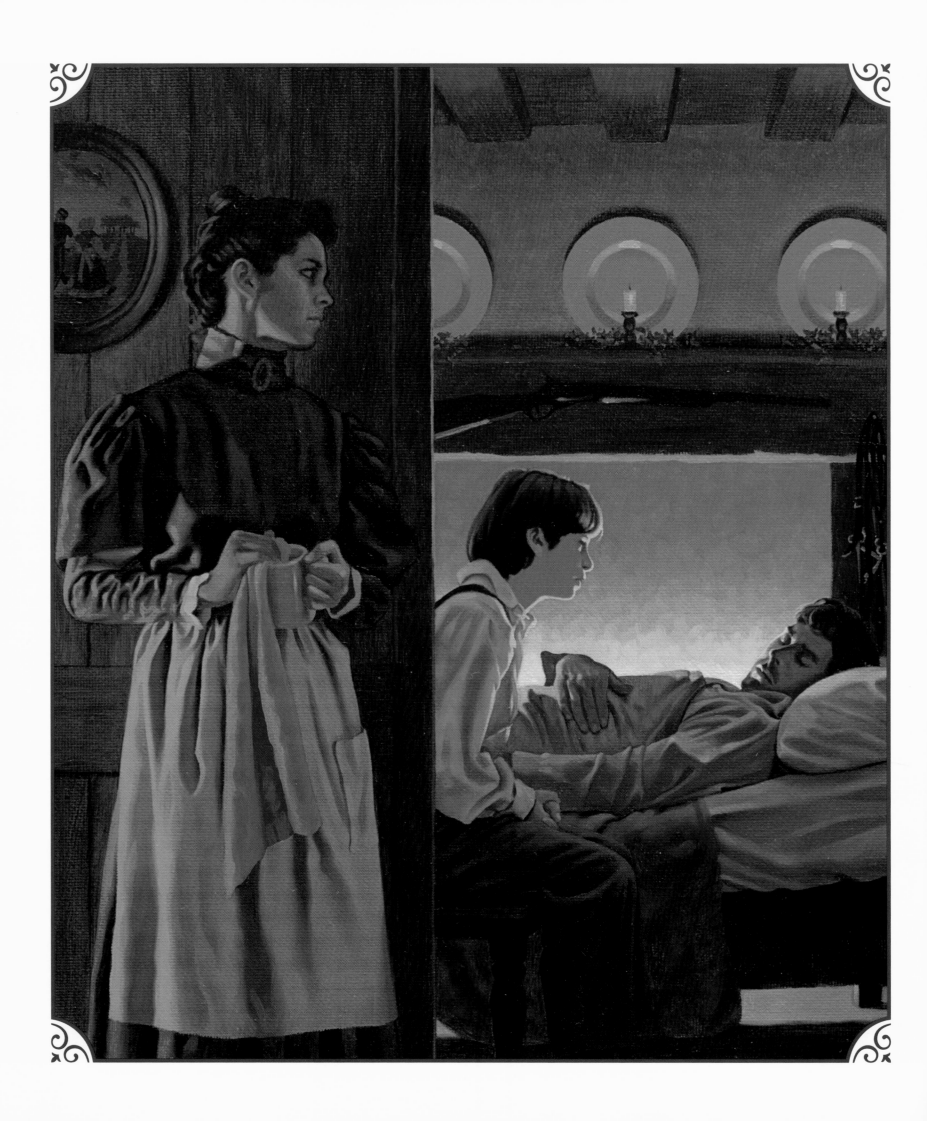

They returned to the ranch and laid the cowboy on a bed by the fireplace.

When Evan tended to the horses, he found the burnished silver bridle. It was beautiful. He had never seen one like it before, so he brought it in, and hung it on a hook by the mantle.

"It will make Cully feel better when he wakes up," he explained to his ma.

The cowboy grew worse that night, and his fever soared. He didn't know where he was, and he talked without knowing what he was saying.

All through Christmas Eve, Evan kept watch, refusing to go to sleep. "If I'm with him, he won't die," he told his ma.

Hoping to break the fever, Della prepared a syrup of willow bark and spooned it into the cowboy's mouth. She laid warmed cloths on his chest to loosen his cough and wiped his brow with rags dipped in cold pine-needle tea.

Christmas Day arrived but it wasn't celebrated at the ranch. Still, Evan was thankful. His prayer had been answered. Cully was home, and he'd made it through the night.

In the following months, the cowboy slowly began to return to health. Evan's ma encouraged him to take short walks with her in the sun. Even so, he was weak, and he slept a lot.

One morning, Evan awoke to find the cot put away and the cowboy's blankets neatly folded.

"He's moved back to the bunkhouse," his ma said. "He wants to take care of himself, and help you when he can."

The house felt empty and strange without the cowboy around. And though Evan and his ma sat by the fire every night, Cully didn't come in and join them.

"He's different, Ma," Evan complained. "He never laughs anymore, and when we're doing chores, he doesn't want to talk."

"Sometimes when a man gets that sick," Della said, "it changes the way he looks at things."

Then one day in early spring, Evan's ma broke the news.

"Cully's made up his mind to quit the trails. He's going into business with his friend Hames. They want to be partners on a big ranch down in Mexico. It's the opportunity he's been looking for."

"He can't leave me behind," Evan said. "It's not fair!"

"That cowboy's been a true friend these past few years," his ma said with a frown. "We should be grateful, son. Now let's both go tell him we think it's a fine idea."

Evan knew she was right, still he didn't like it. Tears welled up in his eyes, but he fought them back. Grabbing the silver bridle off the hook where it had hung since Christmas Eve, he ran ahead to the bunkhouse.

He found the cowboy packing his gear.

"Don't forget your bridle," Evan said. "Every caballero down in Mexico will wish it was his."

Sitting down on his bed, Cully closed his eyes and rubbed his forehead. There was a long silence. At last the cowboy cleared his throat, and said, "Keep the bridle, Evan. It's yours. I tried to get it to you for Christmas, but I couldn't make it."

A chill ran up Evan's spine. It was the most handsome bridle he'd ever seen, and any rider would be proud to own it. But he'd nearly lost Cully because of it, and now he was going to lose him again.

Della stepped into the bunkhouse.

The boy tried to say what he was supposed to—but he couldn't.

"Speak up, son," his ma said. Then he remembered Cully's words by the fire: "Sometimes you have to do what has to be done." It was Evan's turn to be brave, no matter what his friend or his ma might say.

"Cully," he said, "Ma told me about that opportunity you have down south with Hames. Well, I've got a better one for you. . . . If you want to be a partner on a ranch, why not be a partner on this one? Ma needs a husband, and I could sure use another pa."

Della's cheeks turned bright red, and Cully's eyes grew wide with wonder. They all looked at each other. No one knew what to say.

Time passed and in the late spring, when bluebonnets sprinkled the prairie, Della and Cully were married by Lucky Lefty, the cowboy preacher.

All the horses attended the ceremony, but Evan's wore the burnished silver bridle. It turned out to be an even better Christmas present than the horsehair rope. And in the fall when cowboys stopped by the ranch, the boy had his own story to tell by the roaring fire.

Their ranch prospered, and the new family kept a vow they had made on the wedding day.

Every year on Christmas Eve, Evan would lead the way up to Lone Pine Ridge, where they would celebrate, under the stars, a cowboy Christmas.

STORYTELLER'S NOTE

The inspiration for *A Cowboy Christmas* sprang from my interest in the life and times of American women pioneers of the West. My research led me to read many women's diaries and journals of this period. From these I gained a deep respect for the difficulties encountered by not only the women and men of those times, but also by the children. Like the adults, pioneer children had to learn to be brave in order to survive the difficulties of life on the frontier.

There are numerous accounts of widowed women who raised their families single-handedly. Many also ran their own farms, ranches, newspapers, inns, bakeries, and other prosperous enterprises. The major cause of death for cowboys was not (despite what Hollywood portrays) Indian warfare or gunfights, but rather pneumonia. Rampaging prairie fires, cattle stampedes, lightning strikes, rattlesnakes, and bears were all dangers encountered by cowboys. Indeed, life on the trail was such an unhealthy occupation, cowboys rarely survived past the age of thirty.

A Cowboy Christmas is a tribute to the courage and faith of the men, women, and children who braved the many hardships of the frontier West.

—Audrey Wood

PAINTER'S NOTE

A Cowboy Christmas presented me with the opportunity to create some of the most moving images of my illustration career. Unlike the hard-edged technique of many of my previous illustrations, these works are looser and more painterly, in a stylistic cross between Frederick Remington and N. C. Wyeth. The steely blues and grays of the panoramic landscapes provide a dramatic backdrop for the determined cowhand as he faces the cold, stark winters of the American Southwest. In contrast, homey ranch house scenes, awash with the lustrous golds and ochres of the hearths and hearts within, reflect the glowing warmth of the mother and child and their promise of family. And not to be forgotten, the will of nature is an ever-present factor in *A Cowboy Christmas.* From the cold wind and biting snow of winter to the breezy warmth of the eventual spring, the weather plays as pivotal a role in this story as the characters of Evan, Della, and Cully.

—Robert Florczak

THE PAINTINGS FOR

A COWBOY CHRISTMAS: THE MIRACLE AT LONE PINE RIDGE

WERE RENDERED USING OIL PAINT ON CANVAS.

THE TEXT TYPE WAS SET IN 17-POINT LoTYPE LIGHT.

THE DISPLAY TYPE WAS SET IN LoTYPE LIGHT.

THE SECONDARY DISPLAY TYPE WAS SET IN COPPERPLATE 33BC.

DESIGNED BY PAUL ZAKRIS

COLOR SEPARATIONS WERE MADE BY PHOENIX COLOR, ROCKAWAY, NEW JERSEY.

PRINTED AND BOUND BY PHOENIX COLOR IN THE UNITED STATES OF AMERICA

ON 80# PATINA MATTÉ PAPER.

THE JACKET WAS PRINTED ON 80# TOMAHAWK PAPER.

PRODUCTION SUPERVISION BY LISA FORD